COUNT OFF, SQUEAK SCOUTS!

by **Laura Driscoll** • Illustrated by **Deborah Melmon**

A02065543

THE KANE PRESS / NEW YORK

For Eli and Clara, my pint-sized editors
—LD

Text copyright © 2013 by Laura Driscoll
Illustrations copyright © 2013 by Deborah Melmon

Library of Congress Cataloging-in-Publication Data

Driscoll, Laura.
Count off, Squeak Scouts! / by Laura Driscoll ; illustrated by Deborah Melmon.
p. cm. — (Mouse math)
"With fun activities!"
Summary: When Albert the mouse, his big sister Wanda, and the other Squeak Scouts go on a field trip to the attic of the People House, Albert not only learns how to line up in numerical order, he also finds a souvenir for his collection. Introduces the concept of number sequence.
ISBN 978-1-57565-524-6 (library reinforced binding : alk. paper) — ISBN 978-1-57565-525-3 (pbk. : alk. paper) — ISBN 978-1-57565-526-0 (e-book)
[1. Mice—Fiction. 2. Souvenirs (Keepsakes)—Fiction. 3. Scouting (Youth activity)—Fiction. 4. Sequences (Mathematics)—Fiction.] I. Melmon, Deborah. II. Title.
PZ7.D79Cou 2013
[E]—dc23   2012025476

1 3 5 7 9 10 8 6 4 2

First published in the United States of America in 2013 by Kane Press, Inc.
Printed in the United States of America
WOZ0113

Book Design: Edward Miller

Mouse Math is a trademark of Kane Press, Inc.

Visit us online at **www.kanepress.com**

Like us on Facebook
facebook.com/kanepress

Follow us on Twitter
@KanePress

Dear Parent/Educator,

"I can't do math." Every child (or grownup!) who says these words has at some point along the way felt intimidated by math. For young children who are just being introduced to the subject, we wanted to create a world in which math was not simply numbers on a page, but a part of life—an adventure!

Enter Albert and Wanda, two little mice who live in the walls of a People House. Children will be swept along with this irrepressible duo and their merry band of friends as they tackle mouse-sized problems and dilemmas. (And sometimes *cat-sized* problems and dilemmas!)

Each book in the **MOUSE MATH**™ series provides a fresh take on a basic math concept. The mice discover solutions as they, for instance, use position words while teaching a pet snail to do tricks or count the alarmingly large number of friends they've invited over on a rainy day—and, lo and behold, they are doing math!

Math educators who specialize in early childhood learning used their expertise to make sure each title would be as helpful as possible to young kids—and to their parents and teachers. Fun activities at the end of the books and on our website encourage children to think and talk about math in ways that will make each concept clear and memorable.

As with our award-winning Math Matters® series, our aim is to captivate children's imaginations by drawing them into the story, and so into the math at the heart of each adventure. It is our hope that kids will want to hear and read the **MOUSE MATH** stories again and again and that, as they grow up, they will approach math with enthusiasm and see it as an invaluable tool for navigating the world they live in.

Sincerely,

Joanne Kane

Joanne E. Kane
Publisher

Check out these titles in
MOUSE MATH:

Albert's Bigger Than Big Idea
Comparing Sizes: Big/Small

Count Off, Squeak Scouts!
Number Sequence

Mice on Ice
2D Shapes

The Right Place for Albert
One-to-One Correspondence

The Mousier the Merrier!
Counting

Albert's Amazing Snail
Position Words

Albert Keeps Score
Comparing Numbers

And visit
www.kanepress.com/
mousemath.html
for more!

Rosebank

Albert's big sister, Wanda, was helping him with his Squeak Scout uniform.
"Hold still," she said. "I'm almost done. . . ."

4

But Albert was too excited!
It was the day of the Squeak Scout field trip.
They were going to the attic of the People House.
"I can't wait!" Albert told Wanda.
"I'm going to look for a *souvenir*!"

Albert had a collection of souvenirs—
things that reminded him of places he'd been.

There was the funny red cup from the swimming
pool . . .

the hula hoop from the kitchen . . .

and the Frisbee from the backyard.

Albert couldn't wait to find something special in the attic.

"Come on, Albert!" Wanda called. "Time to go!"

They met up with Rachel, Leo, Tim, and their Scout
leader, Agnes.

"The attic is very safe," Agnes said.
"The People never go up there, and the cat can't get in.

"But we need to stay together so no one gets lost."

Agnes passed out safety vests, each with a number on it.
Albert looked down. His number was 2.

"When I call, 'Count off,'" Agnes said,
"line up in order and call out your numbers.
That's how I'll know if anyone is missing."

Rachel, Albert, Leo, Wanda, and Tim
all shouted out their numbers.

Then off they went!
The Scouts scurried along a maze of pipes,
then up a mountain of steps . . .

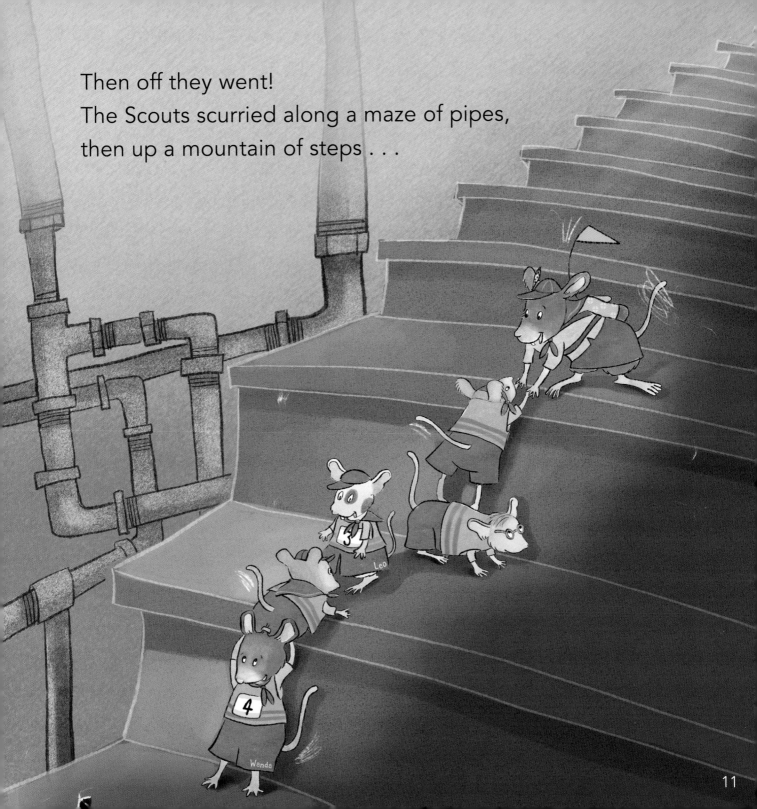

and they were there.
"*Oooooooo*," said Albert, his eyes wide.
The attic went on and on and on!
It was full of wonderful things.

Albert was *sure* he would find something
amazing to bring home!

The Scouts scurried this way and that.
Right away, Rachel raced over to a giant slide.

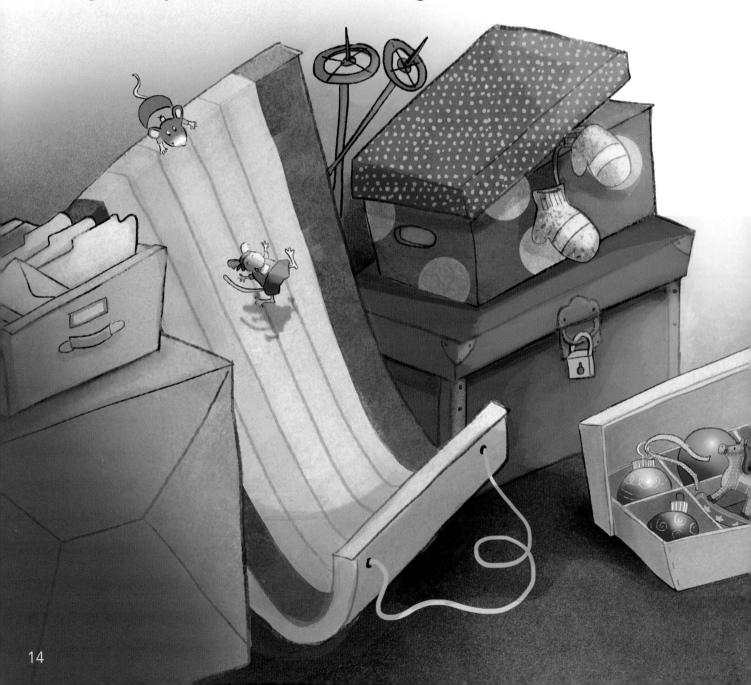

Leo climbed onto a rocking horse.

Albert bumped into a big glass ball.
It was all snowy inside!
But it was *way* too heavy to carry home.

"Count off, Squeak Scouts!" Agnes called out.
The Scouts came running and lined up.

"*Psst*, Albert," said Wanda. "Your number is 2.
"Number 1 comes first. Number 2 comes second."

Albert and Rachel switched places.
"Now we're in the right order!" Wanda said.

The Scouts played Hide-and-Go-Squeak.

Albert saw a cat statue near some boxes.
He thought about bringing it home,
but decided it would give him bad dreams.

They found a merry-go-round.
It was a little fast for Albert.

"Count off!" called Agnes. "Last one here is stinky cheese!"
The mice stopped spinning and lined up.
Everyone was dizzy—especially Albert.

Agnes looked at them. "You're all in backwards order! Try again."

The Scouts changed places. Wanda whispered,
"Albert, 2 goes between 1 and 3."

Albert found his place between Rachel and Leo.

As they explored, Albert kept looking
for his special something.
But there were so many other things to do!

The Scouts bounced across a field of bubbles.

BOING!

BOING!

POP!

They tried on fancy hats in a mouse mansion.

"Count off, you fashion stars!" called Agnes.
The Scouts lined up.

"Where's Albert?" said Wanda. "AL-BERT?"

Albert was thinking.
He counted to himself.

Then he zipped right into place.
"Albert!" Wanda said. "You've got it!"
Albert was very pleased . . .

until Agnes said: "O-KAY! Time to go!"

"Wait! I haven't found my souvenir!" said Albert.
But the Scouts were marching on.

"Aw, rats!" he said. He ran to catch up and
stumbled over a red bump in his path.

A second later they all heard—
Beep . . . beep . . . beep . . . beep . . .

The mice slowly turned and . . .

FLASH! There was a blinding light.
Some of the mice froze. Others dove for cover.

But nothing else happened until . . .

a white paper slid out from the black
box Albert had stepped on.
Slowly, colors and shapes appeared on
the paper—like magic!

"What is it?" Wanda asked.

"It's my *souvenir*!" Albert exclaimed.
It was perfect for his collection—
a magical picture that would always remind him
of the Squeak Scouts' amazing attic adventure.

Count Off, Squeak Scouts! supports children's understanding of **number sequence**, an important topic in early math learning. Use the activities below to extend the math topic and to reinforce children's early reading skills.

ENGAGE

Remind children that the cover of a book can tell them a lot about the story inside.

▶ Invite children to look at the illustration as you read the title aloud. Encourage them to tell what they think the story is about. Ask: *What do you think Squeak Scouts are? How many mice do you see on the cover? What do you think it means to "count off"?*

▶ Before reading the story, talk about what it means to put things in "sequence," or in their correct order. To help children understand the concept, use flashcards with pictures of daily activities (for example: brushing teeth, getting dressed, eating breakfast, etc.). Printable flashcards are available at www.kanepress.com/mousemath-sequence.html. Invite children to help put the cards in order. Ask: *Why do you think doing these activities in order is a good idea?*

▶ Remind children that *numbers* have a correct order too: 1, 2, 3, 4, 5, and so on. Review the flashcards again in sequence, this time numbering each card.

LOOK BACK

▶ After reading the book, encourage children to retell the story in its correct order. Record children's responses on large strips of paper, and tape each strip to the board or a flip chart. Review the resulting story aloud. Ask: *Do you think the story strips are in the correct sequence? How do you know?*

▶ Tell children to listen carefully as you re-read *Count Off, Squeak Scouts!* Ask if they still think their story strips are in the right sequence. Reorder the strips if necessary. Invite children to write a number next to each strip to show the correct number sequence.

TRY THIS!

Squeak Scouts for a Day!

Materials: sequentially numbered cardboard placards (one numbered card for each child, beginning with number 1) on strings so that children may wear the cards around their necks

▶ As children arrive, distribute numbered cards for them to wear throughout the day. Tell them that each time they hear, "Count off, Squeak Scouts!" they should line up in order, beginning with the number 1. When the line is complete, have them call out their numbers in sequence. Work toward having numbers 1–10 line up first; then, numbers 11–20. (Check to be sure that children are in the correct numerical order each time.) By the end of the day (or week) you should be able to say, "Count off, Squeak Scouts!" and have all the children line up in the correct order.

▶ Note: A single child may also try this activity using stuffed animals or other toys or objects. Place a numbered necklace on each animal, and at different times of the day, call out, "Count off!" and have the child put all the animals in their place.

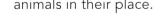

THINK!

Making "How To" Booklets

Materials: Each child will need a pre-made paper booklet, pencils, and crayons.

▶ Invite each child to make a "How To" booklet about one of his or her favorite activities. (Examples: how to ride a bike, how to skate, how to bake a cake, how to play soccer, etc.) Before the children begin, tell them to think about which step comes first, which comes second, and so on.

▶ Have children write or dictate their step-by-step instructions—one page for each step. (Note: Some children may want to draw a picture showing each step.)

▶ Help children number the pages in order.

▶ Finally, encourage children to illustrate the covers of their books.

▶ Invite volunteers to share their "How To" booklets!

◆ FOR MORE ACTIVITIES ◆
visit www.kanepress.com/mousemath-activities.html